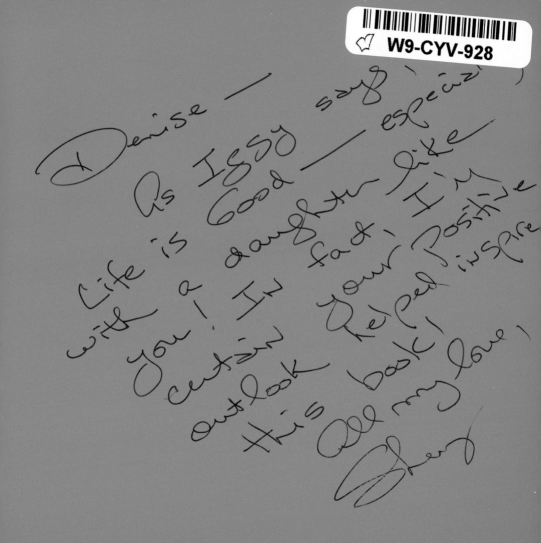

Denise —

As Iggy says —
Life is Good — especially
with a daughter like
you! In fact, I'm
certain your positive
outlook helped inspire
this book!
All my love,
Sherry

The Wisdom of Iggy
The Tale of a Bearded Dragon

Sherry Brosnahan

Photography by Bruce Curtis

**Andrews McMeel
Publishing**

Kansas City

Special thanks to Iggy's friend and trainer, Mariann Zelinski. Mariann is a professional dog trainer with more than fifteen years' experience training dogs for everyday life as well as obedience and agility competitions. She and her husband, Rob, reside in Baldwin Harbor, New York, with their children, Amanda and Amy, two golden retrievers, three rabbits, two guinea pigs, a hamster, some fish, and their beloved Iggy.

05 06 07 08 09 KFO 10 9 8 7 6 5 4 3 2 1

ISBN: 0-7407-5017-8

Library of Congress Control Number: 2004111305

Book design by Desiree Mueller

My Philosophy of Life

By Iggy the Wonder Lizard

People tell me I live a charmed life, and maybe they're right. I often find myself thinking, "Life is good" — mainly because it usually is. I mean, we're talking about life here, right? After all, what's the alternative?

Still, life can throw you some curveballs, and when that happens to me, I just take the good with the good. That's right. Because it's all good. Even an occasional curveball beats the alternative.

Now, there's a real possibility I'm just a lucky lizard. Whenever my luck has been less than stellar, I've managed to hang on to my positive attitude and — voila! — life is good all over again.

And life is even better when you find the right balance. The one that works best for you. The one that lets you enjoy everything life has to offer. Whether I'm hanging out with my friends or just hanging out on a limb, I try to remember my balance.

And that, my friends, may just be the secret to my long and happy life.

All the best,

Iggy

Wise men study their options carefully...

2

pick a career doing
something they love . . .

and still
have time for their
favorite hobbies.

When in doubt, look it up — or just look smart.

Toga party, anyone?

Let your imagination run wild . . .

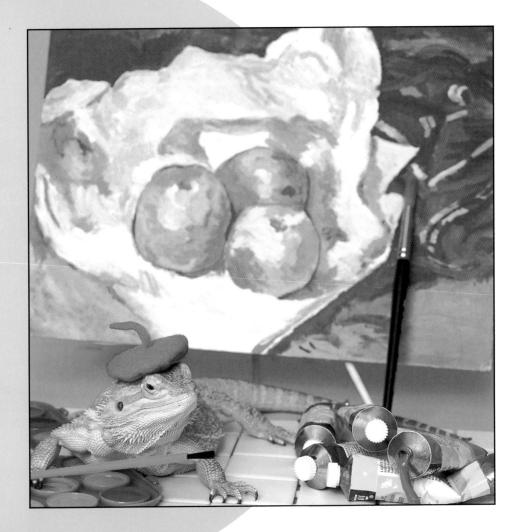

but stay in touch with your gentler, classier side.

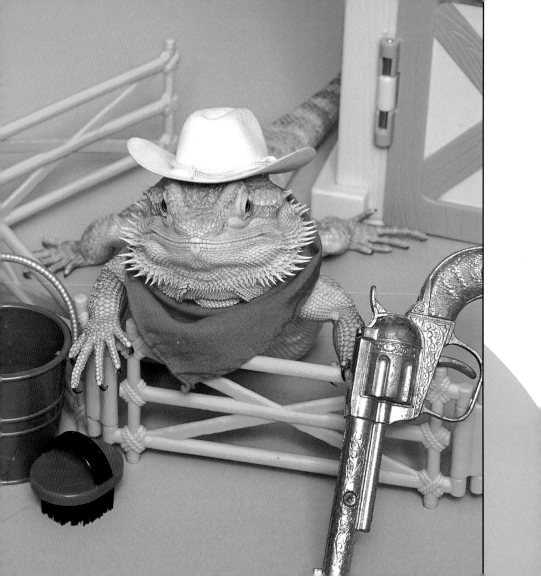

If you can't beat 'em, impress them with your getup.

Iggy's fitness tip:
Find an exercise that
suits your natural
abilities—and have fun!

The best gifts are highly personal and oh-so-special.

To keep boredom at bay, indulge in a little drama . . .

or escape to the
adventure of your dreams.

And always make time for doughnuts.

Look cute, be patient, and you might get out of doing the chores.

It's okay to work hard . . .

when you play hard, too.

you can never be too cool
or too rich.

With wheels like these, who could be a stick-in-the-mud?

The best adventures are the ones you share with friends.

It's soooo good to be king.

Each year brings
more wisdom—and
more partying!

you can carefully chart the course of your life . . .

but allow ample time to goof around with your buddies.

Iggy's health tip:
Gardening is a natural form
of exercise with results that
can be truly edible.

Skip the tricks. Jump right in and enjoy the treats.

Mirror, mirror on the wall, who's the most romantic reptile of all?

If you find yourself out on a limb, relax and enjoy the view.

never miss an opportunity
to enjoy the good life . . .

or to find someone to
enjoy it with.

What are we waiting for?
Let's cruise!

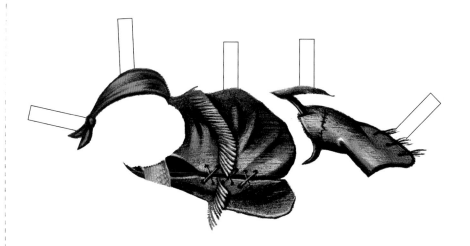